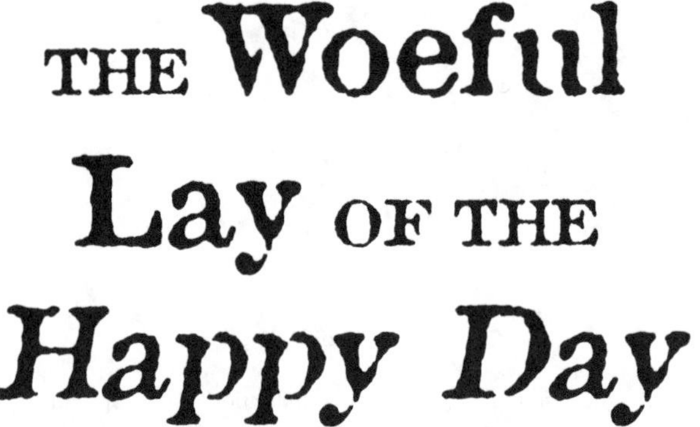

# THE Woeful Lay OF THE Happy Day

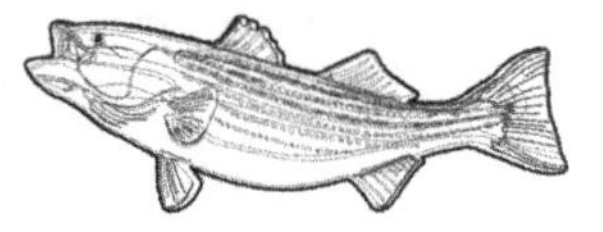

JON SOBEL

This is a work of fiction. Names, characters, events and incidents are the products of the author's imagination. Any resemblance to actual persons, living or dead, or actual events is purely coincidental.

*Book Layout and Cover Design © Roxanne Slimak*
*Jacket and Endpaper Illustrations © Stacey Posnett*
*StaceyPosnett.net*

The Woeful Lay of the *Happy Day* / Jon Sobel – 1st ed.

Hardcover ISBN 979-8-9856500-0-6

# THE Woeful Lay OF THE Happy Day

*—Todos llegan de noche,*
*Todos se van de día…*
*—El amor es tan sólo una posada*
*En mitad del camino de la vida…*

*—They all arrive at night,*
*They all leave during the day…*
*—Love is just an inn*
*In the middle of the road of life…*

- JOSÉ SANTOS
CHOCANO GASTAÑODI

*Upon the steep floor flung from dawn to dawn*
*The silken skilled transmemberment of song;*
*Permit me voyage, love, into your hands…*

- HART CRANE

recked off the shore
of wretched Dead Horse Bay,
Half-bleached, half-rusted, rolled the *Happy Day.*
Child-christened, Mayor-blessed and tourist-loved,
Once motoring island-high, now sunk so low.
Her captain Mary Wragg had axed her down
And therein swims this tale of snow and fire.

Straight out of high school Mary'd struck her path,
To Colorado Springs to seek the sky.
Second Lieutenant seemed a noble start
To a march to orbit, moonshots, and beyond.

She was no slight white thing. Tough as the men,
Red-cheeked, wide-hipped, tiara-ed with yellow straw,
A saxophone among the clarinets
When out with fellow feminine cadets.
Talked fast, thought hard, tired out the lesser souls
Who couldn't run a lap or leap a ditch

Without an overspilling mug of foul
But full-speed coffee from the mess at six.

She never asked how Dover got his name,
Sensing a sore spot, and was keen to ease
The flow of friendship circling in the stiff-
Aired classroom, over the Garden of the Gods,
Along the massif and in the mountain air.
His brain was tuned to charm, his core for climbs,

His trickster spirit sharp and devilish,
Fixing her with a gaze that made her laugh,
A crooked nose and two green lantern eyes
That measured twice, cut once, and she was slain.

Fleeing a buck-brown flood, her brother's children
Ruined their sneakers as neighbors stayed behind.
(Eleven perished.) Sad Cristina steered
Her pipsqueak brother Nathan toward the bus
Their mother'd said she'd be on soon's she could.
Waiting, they smelled the diesel, heard the snap

Of firecrackers set off in the lot
For no good reason, none at all. No reason.

Wragg engineered him into Truman's Pub
One silver October evening sophomore year.
He'd played such tricks himself but played along,
Game and intrigued, a cat with a cicada,

A spy with a suspicion, an elephant
Hurling a log at an electric fence.

"Dover," she said, "I'm over here, look here."
He bought them drinks. They talked of the calculus,
Organic chemistry, topography,
Deepest ambition, unacknowledged fear.

She bought them sliders, sweet potato fries,
Dreaming of a perfect dock, of perfect hair.
"Tonight is not a date," she told herself,
Aware she was pretending not to care.
"Humanities," he bawled. "That's where I'm stuck."
"I'm taking Arabic next year," she told him.

"That's brave." "Oh, I'm all over brave," Mary said.
Dover trembled, his skin all over hot.

They knew each others' ways by Halloween,
The multitudes of freckles on her shoulders,
The mole above his navel. No consent,
No trifling at the gate, no strategy,
No algebra or sage reflection, no
Grave consultation. Just some cheap rosé.

They ran half-marathons at altitude;
Climbed Pikes Peak on an awkward overnight
To gaze at stars, yawn at the vanilla moon,
And spy on satellites; railed to the gnashing

Colorado River to zip and spin
On a neon raft that reeked of plastic light;
Fought a first scuffle in a rented car;
Made up on Cripple Creek; descended deep

Into a gold mine glinting incandescent,
Uncovering the scuttled darknesses.

Finals looming, but turkey break ahead,
Two dozen future officers swapped fates,

Flowering, merging, forgetting who was who,
Surrendering leadership (that virtue so
extolled), extinguishing rank differences,
Grazing together on the starchy commons,
Bloodletting and imbibing, altering states,
Tremendous and unseen and trumpet-loud.

The cold Moon cresting, Dover juicily retched
And passed out on the clay-cooked worm-spun lawn
Beneath a sympathetic quaking aspen
That nodded toward an upper window where

Wragg slumped in one bare bulb's wan slack red light
Knocked silly by two Coors too many, shadowed
By night-shrouded haze from distant fires
That seeped inside insensibly. So she
Had lost the central marble of her focus
That lent her pith to parry the assault.

Hands, one, two hands, three, three, no, four, four hands,
Hands chill and stained with ochre of fool snack
Pressing her—shoulders? neck? Her head of fluff
Smacked into something hard, the room upended.

Arms stocky, stacked with ape-mad muscle. Legs,
Heavy bone chests, ale-checkered knives of breath—
The red ghost glow then suddenly dead bright,
Then suddenly dark. A throb of misty blood

Collapsed one eye. Hands grey with choking fire
Tore into someone close to her, wee girl

Who slithered iced in winter-snot straight down
To kiss the hardwood floor so far below

That no earthly light could reach that golden
Firmament. Yet still the smoldering lamp
Would not wick out complete, however hard
The faerie huffed. She breathed that wee girl's breath,
She sucked it in, squeezed her stuttering skull,
Spat, blew, froze, splintered. Faerie breathed no more.

Nathan tugged on Cristina's dampened sleeve.
"Mommy's not coming, is she?" The bus growled.
Two sodden Wraggs shared peanut butter crackers.
The bus swung creakily into the only

Brightly lit four-lane highway in the state.
"I want to see Mom's text again," the boy
Demanded. The girl sighed her phone awake.
"That's it now. Gotta save the battery."
"Where are we driving?" Hours it seemed had passed.
"To the lighthouse of truth," Cristina said.

The fundamental truth, as Mary knew,
She must fix solid in her deadened mind.

The Palaces of Empty burned silver,
The Humid Caverns sank in psychic mold.

The Quaking Hills gasped for the thinning air,
The Bony Foothills hammered at the gate.
The Caged Red Butterfly flitted unseen,
The Scrubbers punched right through the Clock's glass face.

A frozen sheen grew crystal-clean between them.
He flew home to New Jersey for Thanksgiving.
She feigned fear of infection, stayed at school,
Full-fleeced and hatted stamped the campus grounds.

Her suitemate Miss Shania hailed from Yuba.
Her folks had fled gargantuan wildfires
(Again) so for their precious scattered offspring
There was no home to come home to (again).
Old-fashioned card games helped to pass the time
In the freakish-quiet dorm, day into night.

They spoke small, toasted to a firmer world.
Shania's Coors kissed Mary's Red Bull can.

Stuffed up with dream-packed sleep, she'd sworn to wire
All that long night to scrape her fuddled brain
For memories: timing, faces, colors, clothes.
Red diamonds pierced red hearts, pricked her red eyes,
Brute clubs and smoky spades vied, steely-strong,
To hold her hand. Chalk-faced square-shouldered royals

Smoldered a bald "J'accuse" on midnight's wing.
She peeved about the room and told Shania
Her eyes were seeing wrong. "I'm *not* just tired."
"You're hyper, you're hyped-up, that's all it is."

Our Mary rose and spleened across and down,
Red Bull can ringing hollow on the table.

"Want to play video games?" Shania asked.
"No, I'll go to the gym. I'll be all right.
I'm fine." Mary's hand rested on her friend's
Warm shoulder—"Sorry. I'll let you go to bed."

The family football game of ancient rite
Dissolved in the mad mist and snow. Poor lads.

"I like golf better anyway," jibed Dover's
Uncle Zed, the clan's richest man
Whose sporting goods store closed just twice a year,
On Christmas Day and Ronald Reagan's birthday.
Sisters, brothers, cousins, turkey salad,
Leftover pie for days, gluttony amok.

Slim cousin Elsie showed them her guitar,
Eyes sparkling at Dover as she played
A strain from Guns N' Roses and an air
From J.S. Bach, then quickly set it down

Owning she had not mastered yet the magic
Box, its six mythic steel strings, its soul.
Full soulful she appeared to him, her elfin
Face and short black hair a china doll's.
(Her mother came from an ancient land called Greece.)
Picturing her beside Mary's beety toughness,

Thought Dover, "I can do better. I should.
Just drink less fast at parties." And besides,

The sullenness Wragg'd suddenly indulged in,
The hinted accusation, the withdrawal,

The soaring pains behind her hooded eyes,
Dry drastic pieces of one dastardly
Feminine puzzle. The dull girls he'd kissed
In high school flashed before him like a skein

Of restless paper dolls, dissolved to ashes
One by one in the sun's golden corona.
Mary'd someway beguiled him to another
March, a deeper step—and now where was she?

Two nights the children spent in the vast holds
Of the sometime conference center in the flatlands.
Terrified Nathan clung to sad Cristina
(Whose once-thick sadness shrank and wicked away).
She awaited him outside the dank men's bathroom
So as not once to lose him in the crowds.

Two days passed. Then their mother came to find them.
So, spent, Cristina spun down sad again.

"Is Daddy coming?" Nathan asked. "Not now,"
Yolanda told them. Keith's deployment never
Lapsed, or so it seemed, since Cuba. Wet
Emotions flowed across their mother's face. The girl
Took note. Mom's visage quickly cleared; the boy
Wrapped pudgy arms around her oatmeal legs.

The ache had faded from her cheek and temple
But the inner immolation fastened tight,
Silenced the deathly metal in the gym

Where Mary sweated solitary not-

so-silent curses on the cracked black bench,
And came about to jet through yet again.
Arithmetic abandoned her, she lost
And lost again her abacus of reps.
Her two eyes fell to schism. Her white legs, blotched
Rose-pink and prickly, pitched her as she rose.

Struck shuddering by her shoulder, the grey mirrored
Wall bounced her a twisted future age

Of steady sag, unsteadiness of gait,
Patchy skin and a belly gone to earth.
Quickly she clamped herself to a machine,
Clawed fingers around a bar and pulled as if
Olympic glory were at stake. Eyes shut,
The cockeyed universe consigned to darkness,

Wragg wrestled her brain to a dragged-out draw.
Portcullis breached—invaders dazzle-floored—
Walls scratched with the nine billion names of nightmare—
Arrows aflame above—she pulled. And harder.

"Don't have to stick to the military, kid.
Degrees in engineering are like gold…
This year it's mold remediation. Hot!
And if you don't like mold, there's fire damage:
Houses, vehicles—you take your pick."
For the first time since tenth grade, Dover knew doubt.

More folks arrived, the huge room seemed to shrink,
Grew stickier, enveined with spiny voices.

People flipped cards on milk crates crowned with Titans
T-shirts. Two old men played chess on a rickety
Travel set from travels long forgotten.
Palettes of bottled water trundled in
Were instantly stripped dry and shimmied out
To make way for sickly-sweet cereal bars.

(No sustenance for the throttled, shaking addicts
Lighting up although it was forbidden,
Torching eagerly toward their personal hells.)
Cristina wished for a game, a Twix, her scooter.

If Mary took the stairs upstairs this time
(To find no succor in the little fridge);
If WiFi had again imploded, leaving
A student with nought but her PDFs;
If study mojo anyway'd spun AWOL,
No focus anywhere in the chill suite,

These all counted for nothing; body frame
Bloodsuckered, brain befogged, emotion-sere,

This Little Piggy'd lost the trail to home,
This sudden duckling angled from the line,
These yellow bristles fissile, chaos-bound,
These wrinkly toes wriggled free of the boot.

Bejeweled Shania, tougher than she looked,
Uncompromising, beast-enticing, rode

The elevator checking for a text,
But wrapped in the grey image of a man
Unbanked, unhoused, unvaccinated too
Most likely, worming by a garden wall

Adjacent to the dorm. How he'd got there
Past the electric fence she couldn't say.

The man lay awkwardly twist-hipped, though still,
Seeming asleep. His shape blazed in her brain
As she gave up on hearing news from home,
Slipped phone into front pocket, slipped inside.

Peeked in on Mary, strewn abed asleep
Still dressed for sweat-work, rose neck bent aside
Very much like the grey-skinned man's long legs.
Didn't look right. Gave her a gentle shake
On a cold bare shoulder. Pained awry, our Wragg
Shook electrically awake. "What is it? What's wrong?"

"Nothing," Shania whispered, dimly shamed,
Hissing from the room. "Go back to sleep."

Useless to worry about a troubled friend,
Much less a castaway too proud to beg,
Too old to rock and roll, too cold to cry;
Her fridge running on empty anyway,

Her spending cash spilled on espresso shots
And bottled water (pricier every day)—
Sweet land of self-sufficiency, God knows.
The spirit of the wild, Shania knows.
The wild flight of the burned-out jetsam thrush.
Earning her wings all on her own, God knows.

The walls closed in on Mary's jumbled dreams
Of buses flooded, doors and windows jammed,

Old friends from elementary school trap-doored,
Her rescue crew gone clueless in the cockpit.
The ground fell away; her wee lost F-16
Rocketed into space loaded with babies.

Much like a dream, life leaves you dangling on
A fragile string spun for a lighter load.
Images loathe to coalesce lie sweetly,
Hound and confound while you coil on the floor
In your pajamas, wondering what's next,
Unaware your mouth's been hanging open,

Icicles forming on the roof, rough words
Like lichens fixing to your once-lithe tongue.

Her other mates returned; he would be too.
No text or call, though, all that Sunday long.
On Monday she collared him after Physics.
"If you know who, you better fucking tell me."

*Why can't the past be past?* Dover demanded
Of no one but himself, breaking her hold
And striding—slinking?—storming off, head held
High, ego drooping, snorting like a pig,
Chill as a snakeskin, blinkered like a horse,
Stinking and stealthy like a hungry bear.

The science had escaped her, and she skipped
Right out on Officership that afternoon.
"Warrior ethos" grew a novel meaning.
Warthogs and war pigs mingled in the sun

On fresh-cut grass the color of his eyes,
Warlocks, specters and liches dancing on the sward
Without bending a blade. Warrior ethos
Filled her cup to bursting but the foe
Eluded every sense, even its odor
Splashed away, the grassy volatiles

Subsuming all. Why not let these flat fields
Grow wild? Why waste the watering water?

Wasn't there a shortage? Wasn't there
Almost a war last year over the river?
What did a body mean when flesh was said
And done away with? Who would read this book?
Why did she care? Cottony clouds above
Passed innocent across the sky but they

Were not the sky. The sky remained the sky.
Weakened, imagined as a weightless cloud,
Her dread new demon seemed bestable now.
Skipping one class wouldn't ruin her grades. Sometimes

Self-care took precedence, so wise folks said.
So, shouldered free, she headed toward the gate,
Counting her deep cool breaths—and there were two
Square crewcut boys bright-vivid from the party.
The one cocked Wragg a glance, looked fast away,
The other did not pause his disquisition.

Gravel and cava suckered up her throat,
A goosebump tingle shuddered down her legs,

Today and that Red Day churned, salty soup
Where dark Unknowing chained his briny bride.

A semi screech-howled past, a giant logo
Blazoned on its side proclaiming snacks
For legions. But the man-wide letters split,
Relinquishing their forms before her eyes.

Blinking, she leaned against the nearest wall.
Breathing came ragged. Even the friendly clouds
Had lost their drifty way, prisming like diamonds
On the sand. The gummy stones she stood on
Buckled, comical and blank like clay.
School was suddenly a wispy dream.

Tears formed and welled but the hard floodgates held.
Electric fury sizzled, misting any

Suspended water vaporous to the air.
The almost-winter chill burned likewise off
Her pink now-steamy skin. Papery leaves
Circled—*Mater Suspiriorum*—by her feet.

"Is Daddy on the phone?" When Nathan tugged
On blue Cristina's sleeve she whirled upon him.
"Quit it, pest. She's not talking to Daddy.
Daddy'll be home when he gets home.
And we'll be home too. Go. Leave me alone."
He shrank off, sidled closer to Yolanda

Who wore a hopeful shine on a shaded face.
"We might be going home tomorrow, *changuitos*.

Come pray a little more, so we'll be sure."
"I have to pee." "Go with your brother." "I *know*."
"When you get back we'll pray." "The line's so l*ong*."
"God will wait." "And make *us* wait,"
Cristina said too softly to be heard.
"I hate this line. Why isn't there a line

For kids? A special bathroom just for kids!"
"There should be. Filled with candy. I'll suggest it,"
Cristina said, "to the authorities."
"I *hate* oh-thorities." "You're such a baby.

Do you even know what 'authorities' means?"
"Yes I do. Like that song Grandpa likes.
I fight them, when I fight them, when I fight
Oh-thority oh-thority always win."
"Nobody *always* wins," Cristina said
With focused mien and older sister wisdom.

She felt her head all around. The lump was down,
The sores evaporated. And she felt

Her skull in front: a forehead hot with sweat,
Though wintry pangs waved past with urgency
The calendar endeavored to deny.
A nose a little doughy, like the upper
Arms no count of reps could tone enough.
Cheekbones some had admired, said were good

As if to single out an element
That carried hope of raising all the rest.
Features all decently in order, save the

Eyes, that though pooled in ancestral places

Would coordinate no more, larimars
That flashed a happy cadence at the start
Of any new adventure, eyes that darted
From dear friend to friend through high school clamors
Like the piercing headlights of a car,
Leading the way often as not or pulling

A reluctant smile to a fresh abyss
Of joy. But here the asphalt kept its secrets.

Companions, scattered rough along Ike's roads,
Reduced to specters in triumphant Tim's.
Cut down she rankled home, where even the faces
Of her suitemates took weird alien tilts.

Their mild familiar colors, odors, calls,
Their dusky surfaces and stabs of brilliant
White, their serious prattle, closet glam,
Cracked laughs and scratchy moans—"Another essay?"—
Bitten-off curses, blasted incantations,
Their howls of outrage, shrieks of pure delight,

Snatches of barrio, tales of city nights,
Tornado mornings, shamed retreats, bald lipstick

Conquests—all these slid off her bruised pink shell.
She pined for her old room—the ukulele
She could barely play, the dungeon smiles
Of Lindsey Vonn and Christen Press, the quiet.

Night fell so awfully early now, though there
Was nothing one could do outside the shelter
Anyway. Her mother thanked the Lord
Her Nathan'd whined himself early to sleep
And her Cristina, magically enough,
Had grown up nearly old enough to talk to.

Cristina's thoughts cast anywhere but Mom
Though. "Can I call Daddy? My phone's charged."

"I told you don't be bothering anyone
Right now," Yolanda said. "You'll waste your juice."
"Well can I call *somebody*?" "Do you need
To call so many people? Just be quiet."
*I shouldn't talk to her like this*, Yolanda
Scourged herself, but couldn't modulate.

And still the girl refused to leave it be.
She asked if she could call her best friend Kim,
Or last year's best friend, the dyslexic one,
Or Grandpa Matías, MIA for ages.

"What if I just call Auntie Mary? Mom,
Can I call Auntie Mary? *Auntie Mary*?"
"Don't hassle Auntie Mary, she's at school."
Cristina stormed away toward the ladies'.
Chewing the second half of her charity
Baloney sandwich, Mama spat and seethed.

As midterms loomed he liked to get away
And rock his brain into civilian places.

Black Bear seemed right. The diner air hung still
And feathery, redolent of grease
And soup and stainless steel, his books
And tablet stacked beside a lukewarm cup
Of mediocre coffee and a chicken wrap
Upon a tastefully chipped white plate.

One local girl made waiting tables something
Of an art, so graceful yet constrained
By a faint hesitant shy mystery.
Her black hair and red lips reminded Dover,

Reminded him, reminded him of something,
Someone. Someone who hid the moon and shamed
The flowers. A phantom form-shifter. His blood
Leaping over boundaries, hounds unleashed,
He smiled and shook his head, fingered the tablet
To glorious life like Christmas, eye-summoned

A coffee refill without a raise of the arm
Or a word. A boy; a conjuring hero.

Tablet ablaze, slashing through finals, Wragg
Dove into winter break like Crazy Jane,
Calling down curses on the naked heads,
The fuzz-topped heads, the Hammerheads
Of Earth, heads everywhere directing
Evil, livid, vile, and shameful acts,

Imprinting their unstoppable command
Straight up the mewling maw of happenstance,
That soft black hole, that slacker, that fat chance

Where numbers undercut you from within.

A numbers game, the number of the beasts,
Innumerable, irrational, ill-timed,
Insatiable, implacable, unsound—
Numbers unnumbered, unbound, ugly, vain—
A jacuzzi full of numbers set aboil
To suck you under, tubes and roots and all.

"Five trillion dollars on the last two wars."
She read the numbers, tried to comprehend.

A sweet new little shadow trailed her now.
The house bubbled with unaccustomed noise,
With kitchen clatter, giggles, whines, and spills.
One minute blue Cristina glided sure,
Rod-straight of back with angel gait to show
Maturity beyond her years to Auntie,

The next she tumbled down the grassy yard,
Crunching the last few fallen leaves, yowling
As twigs and pebbles pressed into her skin
And laughing like a foaming pool of rapids

While Nathan fluttered like a firefly,
Running out to the yard to scan the sky
For any hint of snow, though Mary explained
That like the last, this winter wasn't much
Of one. But Nathan never had seen snow.
Upstate New York held other wonders, yes—

The gorges, lakes, the vineyards—a square house
With a sloping yard, hedges, forest behind,

And dry—dry floors, dry walls, history intact.
A granddad too, not Daddy, but still a man
Who joked and swung his weird white-yellow hair
And seemed to like the company of little

Thieves. Craig was his name, Craig Wragg. Cristina
Loved to flip those syllables about
Her radioactive superhero tongue.
Of Mrs. Wragg they saw much less. A quiet
Grandma who cooked but disbelieved in salt
Or sweets, read library books on an ancient Kindle

And seemed interested only in the boy
And even that a trifle grudgingly.

At least he was a reader, not like sad
Cristina—who felt much less blue these days
Ensconced in a new world of chill excitement.
Auntie and niece resplendent, one in clarion-
Orange fleece, the other tucked inside
A battered bomber jacket that belonged

In olden times, so Grandpa swore, to her
Own Daddy, said "Au revoir" to the listing
Fake Christmas tree festooned with slate-red balls,
And sailed out on a tramp to Ice Cream Island

"Where Toppings Meet the Tropics." Don't forget:
For little Nathan double chocolate. Melted? So?
So what that it's December? Kids deserve
The treats that thrill their spirits all year long.
Secretly Mary thanked the flood that sent
These Christmas-miracle elves to tug her arm

And steer her thoughts away from darker dens
Where creatures of much fouler magic dwelt.

Good Mama-practice too, with theirs back home
Scrounging the soaked detritus of a house,
Constructing fresh conundrums for a family
To one day soon re-gather to address.

"Good Mama-practice"—three words quaintly thought,
Then quickly coiled to a scorpion sting:
These borrowed children might engorge a fancy,
Might jolt lapsing momentum of the mind,
Might even conjure visions of a brood
Of Mary's own. But true companion mojo

Seemed to her now a bruised and barren chant
Of facile lyrics set to broken chords.

Even as she held Cristina's hand
Amid the ice cream parlor's sugary smell,
Her heart began to froth and gurgle. When
It came their turn to order, all words fled.

The childishly handwritten list of flavors
Looked like a fishing net of wriggling sea mice;
Could she have read the words, she still could not
Have spoken to the scooper to deliver
The order she'd affixed securely to
The lattice in her head moments before.

"Ma'am?" chirped the scooper—a teenage
Red-cheeked-girl besmocked in dulcet stains.
*Am I a "Ma'am" already? Can she see*
*From my dulled face the age now printed here?*

The unwelcome word, the thought, rasped her awake.
The flavor recitation trickled, word
By word, back into Mary's frozen skull.
Too late; her not-so-sad resourceful niece
Grasped something blown askew in Auntie's stance
Always as solid as a puck yet now

As shaky as a cookpot full of coals.
Cristina gave the order. "Make it so."

The kids and Mom in bed, Craig settled with
A glass or three of modest Pinot Gris
To lose himself in ancient movie fare
Of eeriness and horror. Daughter Mary
Angled down the concrete stairs to where
She'd cushioned off a damask cellar den,

Content to lend her shivery upstairs room
To Nathan and Cristina. In the muffled

Stillness there she thought to text Denise,
Her high school friend who'd clung to her old childhood
Home despite the feuding folks who fed her
Cookies by the bag. Composed a phrase

But left it hanging at the small screen's edge,
Edge which had doubled, shed its kilter for—
For an unknown dimension solely lit
Lit by a lightning-sharp white flash, then tucked
Tucked back into sliced darkness where a girl
A girl tried fruitlessly to see the whirlwind.

The black-haired Black Bear server greeted him
Smiling a summer storm next day. He ducked

His head with native bashfulness, just so.
Name-tag Vanessa, lipstick red. Eyebrows
Plucked cool, demeanor warm. Vanessa.
Name that can't be shorn, always Vanessa.

He'd timed it right. Shift over, apron off,
Coat on. But at the door: a reedy boy
To meet her, backwards baseball cap, weak beard.
As Dover puffed a laugh over his plate
The glass door shut behind the pair. He faced
His late-night turkey sandwich once again.

The stomach never failed him, always true.
Devoted friend. The brain, and other parts,

Much less dependable. Plenty of fish
In town though. Gang of teenage giggling girls
Steeping in ganja in the parking lot
This very moment. Underage and in

A public place under the smoky stars
But free as bats gobbling mosquitos. One
At least was sure to gravitate, look there,
To a fit and green-eyed officer in training.
Lamplight glanced and vapor danced along
The length of Dover's stalwart crooked nose.

The engine revved, the gearshift shook and hove.
Here Dover dangled, sober as a stone.

A short and sturdy-walking brown-haired girl

Snug in a sleeveless ice-blue vest of down
And silent as a bone side-eyed him like
A lovely beetle on a balcony,

Reminding him of nobody at all!
This glorious feeling! This uncommon find!

Not sure of her *anima* after all,
But soft, with skin that dreamed by like a cloud,
She smelled of different flowers—which he kept
About him all the next day, scent that served

To steel his wavering XY carnivore.
But all for nought. He saw no sign of Wragg.
Not like her to cut class. He thought to text
Shania, but not wanting to be thought
A fool, he held his thumbs. She'd reappear
When she saw clear to show herself again.

Quickly the new semester filled with clutter
He waded through with muttering resolve,

Till, one week gone, it smacked him the face:
Mary had not returned to school at all.
Had something gone down over Christmas break?
Had those beams in her eyes got stuck awry?

"Take the old van—your mother needs the car.
Just got it tuned up. Look, new tires too.
You paint a flower, look just like a hippie.
You'll take my debit card—gas is expensive.

Futon inside, in case you get stuck someplace.
But just make sure the kids put on their seatbelts.
I know you'll be fine, after all who taught you
How to drive? Your old man, that's who, right?"

So, loaded up with sandwiches and Gatorade,
Granola bars and water, seedless grapes,
The clothes and toys the children had arrived with,
And Nathan and Cristina peering out
The too-small windows, the old Wragg family van
Embarked on yet one more adventure, steered

By the future Air Force pilot Craig had wrought,
Whose future was mutating by the minute,

Though Auntie Mary wore the hero's mantle
This late December morning on the hill
Cloud-shrouded, hoarfrost-flecked but scarecrow-dry,
The slope she had slid down in winter, rolled
In summer, raked in autumn, watered in
The spring—picturing fire trucks' fiery wails—

She'd never dreamed of cutting foreign throats.
She'd drop the kids back home in Tennessee,
Kids like all those whose bright lives she had meant
To make her life's work laboring to shield.

Two days rubbering along grey highway flats
Smiled by like boardwalk holidays. A night
In a wan crumb-freckled diesel-fumed motel
Stoked past in beaming colors, a parade
Of stolen sights and smells and Coke machines
And crunch of glass beneath their boots outside.

Next afternoon in soggy Tennessee
Yolanda's citrus smile of sweet relief

Hooked them with happy welcome. Mary stayed
One night to help move furniture. Though all
They'd squirreled in the cellar was no more,
The children could take to their rooms again
Where blue Cristina swallowed back the urge
To ask if there'd been news of Daddy's leave.

As Mary spoke her bittersweet goodbyes
Cristina hugged her tight, but Nathan shrank.
Yolanda kissed her. "Thank your folks and thanks
To you too. Hope that beast holds up for you."

She beasted home in one confounding day,
Thirteen squished hours, just two stops for gas,
The tank grazing the void near midnight when
Those four fresh tires rolled up the Wraggs' green knoll
Just touched with white dust flaking from the air,
A taste of winter (though next morning gone).

Aim: New York City. Land of everything
And all and none. Land of no-matter-what.

Of wishful winds and fish-full waters, flensed
To an *obbligato* churn by fleets of ferries.
Metropolis magnificent aswarm
With rooftop honeybees, distilleries
Behind brown stable doors, olfactory
Malevolence dispelled by ganja grace.

Athwart one ancient block a Shropshire lad,
A hollow man, a love supreme, songs from
A wood, baskets of kisses, cast iron kids,
A mistress coy, apples and quinces,

Elms of death and pear tree ghosts shoulder
To shoulder with bright golden domes of life
Circled by well-fed hawks oblivious
To all the helicopters of the dawn.
Stone towers, glass-eyed spindles, haunted bricks,
Doughboys of bronze, jade buddhas, stinking masks.

Blessed exhaustion purified our Wragg's
Midnight agenda, cleansed her rising mind.

A minute, maybe two, skimmed by and then—
And then buzzcut damnation thundered in,
A white-hot lightning strike behind the eyes.
Orange and green electron sparkles blitzed
Her woolly grey synapses, clogged her lungs,
Tilted her eyes one from the other. *It's my eyes,*

*They're only overtired from those looping,*
*Timeless miles of these United States.*
The thought was sterile as outer space. She knew it.
*The eyes, but not the eyes.* The body shook

Minutely, the jaw clamped, and fury welled.
No more diversions, niece and nephew home
And Christmas over, Jesus come and gone,
The rotten underbelly of the rood
Exposed to all the populace, heathens
Attuned to Mary's carapace of shame.

The ping-pong of Denise's text splashed in
Her second cup of Craig's muddy-black brew.

*first night in nyc you in? we're crashing*
*at my cousins. u gotta believe*
*its new years eve gf! u know u wanna.*
The subdued celebration Mary'd planned—
Fireworks over the lake with Mom and Dad,
Then home to watch the ball drop on TV—

Now felt like a despicable retreat.
"You want to take the van?" Craig asked. "You two
Are getting along so well, it's nice to see."
Mary declined and booked a bus seat. "Much,

"Much better, I think," pursed her mother softly.
A mother's worry is a wondrous thing,
Fantastical, instinctive, raw, sublime.
This mother's only daughter gave her hives,
Conniptions sucked-inside, hot stomach acid.
Mom's dictionary spurned all fighting words.

Though former Mary surely would have driven,
Contemporary Mary'd had a vision:

A road flipped upside-down, herself inverted,
Eyes wobbling like marbles in a mine,
Bones on the outside, skin and sweat within,
The moon blindingly bright, the sun a cooling
Coal after a crackling barbecue
Long blanched into the bowl of memory.

She never would have said this, but in truth
She simply did not trust herself to drive

Another rattling kilometer.
This alien lack of confidence knocked her cold.

Bus station: need address. Response froth-jittery:
Numbered street, Astoria, Queens. *but i thought*
*u were in nyc. j/k.* Her burst
Of thumb-type joking pulled a sheepish smile
Up toward her nose, but only for a split
Before a shroud of knowing curtained down.

*plenty of space* Denise thumbed back.
*sleep in the tub ok? k cu soon*

No time to wait for answers had Denise.
Maybe she would be just the right distraction
To stay our Wragg's fell tumble—she, her cousin,
And the raging chaos of First Night
Was New York Fuckin City in the wet
New age of storms, aborted expectations,

Soupy arrases of pumpkin haze.
The trick, our Mary wrote between the lines
That gonzoed by on cloudy 81,
Is yes to go along and hit whatever

Stoned celebration that awaited her,
Stay sober, and remember humans aren't
All evil all the time, no matter what
Outcry her organ orchestra let loose
To counterpoint and fanfare out the small
And meek and lonely kindly thought.

Faint smell of rocket summer down below
Snipped out the cold and noisy breeze above.

Like a ribeye steak the N train rumbled in.
Packed platform, people wrestling through the doors,
All spider-faced and grumbling at the wait.
A train crew shortage once again, or so
The app declared, but Mary didn't have
The app. Cooking her cud at her own slow boil

She sank into the subway lullaby:
A steel-wheel shriek, a fat-man-spread, a pile
Of thrown-up rice and beans, three gender-fluid
Someones talking loudly in an angled

Slang Mary could barely understand,
A faded t-shirt: *Pain heals. Chicks dig scars.*
*Glory lasts forever.* Hallelujah.
A subway neophyte Mary was not,
Not quite. An unexpected jolt of awe,
Though, struck her—could it be a tiny bit

Happily?—that weird moment when the train
First poked its sooty nose into the sky.

There stood the stern Manhattan monoliths
Arrayed across the river, a phalanx
Of glinting gladiators, armor of brass
And visages of stone, lank silhouettes
Framed by a whitened firmament of ash.
The crowd thinned. Orange plastic seats appeared.

Crammed with *gigantes*, feta, baklava,
Dorado, lamb, and mezzes by the pound,
Mary, Denise, Denise's cousin Cele

And Cele's new roommate Shep blitzed snow-clad south

To shocking-blue Long Island City, stuffed
Into an Uber drowned in lavender.
The price gobsmacked our Mary. New Year's Eve
Had never been so damned expensive, no
Big deal when split four ways but OMG.
The neo-hipsters on the loading dock

Dripped meltingly from end to end to end
With neon drinks and fancy cheese, and cakes

And cookies from Italian bakeries
You couldn't find unless you knew the code.
A hopped-up dog adored the revelry
Galloping loose onto and off the wide
Concrete and on and off, a squirrel in
An acorn heaven, rubbing, wagging, warm.

It magnetized to Mary, tickling, vanishing,
Nosing her leg with wet black nose, again
Vanishing like a needle in an arm.
Cele's friends were mostly artsy folks, but one

Tall boy with sandy dark brown hair confessed
To being an app developer who toiled
For NYC itself—sometimes the Parks
Department, right now for the ferries that
Glid up and down the estuaries and
Lately the new canals. Schedules, service

Updates, fares that rose and split and rose
Varying with a person's means and health.

"We are the only city in the country
That does the fares like this." Enthusiasm!
Tentacles flailing almost happily,
Tall pale boy, a stiff gust of harbor breeze.

A dog, a boy, a chill dry *plein air* fest,
Sharp premature crack-booms of fireworks
Illictly imported to the more
Ancient Queens alleys not yet swallowed up
By towers of glass or cubes of ugly brown.
The hour neared, champagne began to pop

In syncopated accents; Wragg accepted,
Bathed in graciousness, a simple plastic flute.

Uncoiled upon a nighttime-filthy chaise
She welcomed to her leg a quivering paw,
A snout that begged to share her cheese and crackers;
Felt for the first time in at least a month
Content and comfortable amid the swirl
Of well-wishes and kisses all around.

The boy, who'd moved on, floated a sweet smile
Her way. Returning it with a distant nod
She scratched the grateful head that asked for nought
But a morsel now and then of something nice.

Imaginings: "Just called to say I miss you."
Stepping down from the party deck to take
The call uncalled, the voice unvoiced, the void.
No plainchant text; the blessed harmony of
A real voice call, so easy to forget
These black-glass slabs still let you talk that way.

Feeling worse for the dog she'd up and left
Than for the Failure-of-a-Boyfriend in

Her mind, she smiled a strained one, imagined touching
The green-glowing button and not the red.
*But I am a mature grown woman. I*
*Have agency, the power to make my life.*
"I got, I don't know, I got no one to be
With New Year's Eve. Guess I just miss you, Mare."

"Hold on." A subway thundered by above,
Taking its cranky time. She'd walk the block,
Then walk it back. "Yo, Dover, it was you
Ditched me, or maybe you forgot."

"I didn't! I just—didn't know what to say.
Or how to talk about—you know." *You know?*
"Dover," she breathed, "this is not a good time."
"Okay, well, I'll just see you back at school,
I guess." "I guess. I can't talk more right now."
"K. Happy New Year." "Happy New Year, dude."

The glowing screen'd rock alien colors, red
And green and white but a nameless non-hue too,

Shadow-steam beneath a misty streetlamp
Angling away from where she thought she'd been;
Embedded nature rising, clambering out
Leaving a carbon sediment to molder
Grey and inert while dream-stuff wandered wide
In colors that no physics she knew knew.

She'd shove her phone into her too-tight pocket.
She'd rub her eyes, drag out the rainbow sparks.

But that would make it worse. She'd stretch her arm
To a friendly gingko tree—but has it moved?
She'd step up to a curb just where it angled,
But it had moved. Angle her fingers to
Her forehead. Her misstep had loosed a gob
Of crinkly saliva. Fantasy over.

She woke after an hour or two of sleep
To the coil of coffee and the crack of eggs.
A tablet on the kitchen counter played
A tale of New Year's weddings on a boat.

Clear picture, tiny sound, omelettes aborning.
Shot her eyes around the room: All clear—
But things not fully integral. *Lack of sleep.*
Caffeine would soothe the chill and right the ship,
Surely a cup of homebrew sloshed inside
Would steady a wild compass needle. Right?

Maybe not as rich as Craig's, but so much better
Than at school—and here the imagined
Voice on the phone last night thudded straight to
The soft wild surface. Colorado felt

So far away—in time as well as space.
The mountains here were only fragile glass,
The sun-streaked Rockies satchels of mere dreams.
New York's indigo tunnels spit the mucky
Oil-spill rainbows on the kettle ponds
Where frogs foregone and urban turtles cruised.

The city raised its colors with a shout;
America hung hopeless on the staff.

The bird of fortune passes everywhere;
The worms of Hades kiss the salmon of hope.
Cloaked in regret the pigs of war rearm;
The wolves of sweet oblivion lie down.
Writhing in Gotham's clammy grip Wragg ran
The RFK and Randall's Island round.

The flaying wind over the bridge turned her
Redder even than she had ever shone.
But, eighteen months attuned to altitude,
She drank the thick cold city air like broth.

The painted metal hammocks of the gods
Arched lofty in balletic majesty
Over the frost-scuffed ballfields and the sheds
Sore pill-addicted Calibans called home.
Broken-board paths fed poisonberry bushes
That dropped their issue to the fish below.

Over a broken fence: a glimpse of two
Wild horses grazing dolefully on grass

That held its dusty green year after year.
Outlying quadrants, now subtropical,
Like island nations squeezed their own muscle
Milk, made their own wetlands, deified
Fondly remembered denizens, defied
The snow god, trash-talked indifferent Zephyros—

Blizzards, windborne sky-filth, rising seas—
Grey avatars of blind destruction stopped,
Shorn of their sharpest claws and spun to song.
"Only look out for bobcats," Cele had warned.

*I'll run this island round,* breathed Cadet Wragg,
*And run it round again, and climb back home.*

A tiny laugh squelched from between her bones.
*Home!*—was a small apartment where she owned
A welcome for just one or two days more,
In a city where the streets were paved with souls,
In a borough where she'd never been before,
On a street without a name, only a number.

She never saw the ferry boy again
But January Second, when there came
A gusty wind that clarified the sky
To a crisp blue-eye blue that almost hurt to look at,

The choppy waters beckoned her. The Finger
Lakes whereon she'd sailed in childhood,
Mouth a grim portcullis of taut wire,
Face and arms sun-freckled, never eddied
Dangerous as spider spit like these did,
Charging up the berms like rabid mustangs

Mouths afoam. Those leisure boats never groaned
So happily as Gotham's raffish ferries.

Crew was a start, Captain could come in time.
Check tickets, operate gates, awaken sleepers

(Projecting military discipline).
As history has proven, leadership
Demands neither true moral vision nor
Sensory confidence. *I am a natural.*

*Illusions and distortions—they're as real*
*As anything I walk on, or a bite*
*Of any hostile insect, or a storm.*
Hark to the trials of Wragg upon the waters.

Sailed murky channels, rippling bays, the yawning
River that still flowed both ways, the new
Canals, the old Charybdis of Hell Gate,
The fisheries of Coney Island Creek,
Cottony quiet at the Navy Yard,
Cacophony amid the Wall Street Piers.

She'd gleaned the turgid depths of Pelham Bay,
Greeted the dolphins along Jacob Riis,

Assessed the Verrazzano, bumped along
The bricks of Ellis Island, braved the rough
Of Dead Horse Bay—though never clocked the poets
Or the Ravine of Central Park. She'd leapt
The stink of the Gowanus, nosed the dunes
Of Breezy Point, skirted the Palisades,

Absorbed the hazards of U Thant but still
The Met and One World Trade remained mere tales.
The attic that she shared near Lakruwana
Steamed tropical. She worked as many shifts

As the service would allow, herding commuters,
Tourists, musicians, humans with no homes,
Learning the flows and eddies, sharp turns, banks,
Top pizza stops, kaleidoculture codes.
Kids mostly, like but not so like the fresh-
Baked leaders back in Colorado Springs.

Naiads cavorting in an algal bloom
Can joust a ferry from her wonted lane.

The gentle rippling calm of MARSEC 1
Can camouflage a pestilential threat
Arising from the deckhand's cobbled bowel,
Packs of marauding Jet Skis in the roar,
A suicidal seal on one last spree—
A wild rotating rainbow of digressions.

A sailor must have more than sea legs and
A hardened stomach, must have too a pair
Of steady eyes fronting a steady mind
To sink a psychic plumb bob to the muck,

Be buoyant, always skipping to the top
With vision sound, sound five-by-five, core bound.
Deckhands must be the docents of the deep,
Guides and pretenders, stout-brained sonneteers
Commanding the recalcitrant, offering
Kind welcome to all good-faith pilgrim hands.

Still, no one blamed a newbie for a stagger.
A girl with misbehaving eyes could fake it.

Besides, the brain adjusted. Adaptable thing.
Could learn to recognize bad news in boys,

Could push persistent guilt aside, could spend
Its last two dollars, sure the bank's to blame;
For sure could learn to keep the portrait straight
In a frame that seemed to angle, thrust, or veer.

Portrait of Mary Wragg: Gone solid with
Her sailing mates—most New York City-born,
Dark-skinned (most Captains too). Mary stood out
Pink and rose-red, freckles in multitudes,

Hair melancholy yellow, shocked, untamed;
Booted, hard-elbowed, shoulders round and just
A little broader than her folks had imagined,
Eyes cool but blinking often, catlike nose,
Her bearing straight, well-regulated, brooked
No nonsense, laughed at jibes and jokes on breaks

But never broke intention on the boat,
Filling the uniform with stainless pride.

Arrived the anniversary in June
Of Craig and Anina's happy little girl's
Emergence. Struck her, turning 21:
No one in her new universe even knew;
No one to celebrate with, take her out;
Only the potted wishes of old friends

On soulless screens, drumbeats from long-gone girls
(And not a single boy), an old-style ring

From Dad and Mom, and, touching—though parent-urged—
A heart-text from "your awesome niece Cristina."

Brother Keith, home for a short time in the spring,
Had been deployed again; this time to help
Volcano refugees St.Vincent way.
Less danger…Still he never called his sis.
But that was fine with her. He only made
Her think of what she'd given up, or what—

She told herself sometimes in stanky mood—
Had been unceremoniously snatched away.

Weary after a late shift, Mary trudged
From St. George Landing toward her bus stop in
The humid night whose air caressed her wind-
Chapped skin with towels of felt. Beer neon beckoned
Left and right. Her molecules felt no
Temptation, but a creeping sadness wafted

Towards her with the gentle movement of
The tepid island air. *Legal to drink,*
But nobody to lift a glass with—in
A city of eight million thirsty souls.

A false and youthful sheen of self-importance
Commanded her to seek more extra shifts,
Accumulating hours upon hours
Hastening her ascendance to command—
For that's where lonely special people feel
Truly and—masked in noble angst—at home.

Conquering a city and its waters all
At once, that's how she'd wrest the sword

From the eternal ribboning grey schist.
As never before she sensed the vulcan truth:
That we are strangers here, the world is from
Of old. To ply its straits, to boldly go
A-maying here in June, to smell the roar
Of time-forgotten bones scuttled offshore,

To hew the yapping boys of summer down,
Cut loose the strange-eyed ladies of the stake—
Our Mary recks the depths, assays the ore,
Aiming to raise the wrecked and win the gold.

Humanities and leadership and physics.
Late nights, dawn reveilles, red tired eyes.
Nearly deserted by the brutal science
He'd fought to master, twisting in the winds
Of poetry and art, he passed his finals
Barely, and with plenty of help at that

From a smart and smartass friend he'd meant to shun
Since the incident with Bragg of Lessened Memory.

Breaking one and then two local-girl hearts
He breezed away to Oregon for a summer
Fighting the fires that threatened the whole human
Population there with snuffing out.

Lightning touched off the one in late July
That drew his team of twenty-six on Day

Fourteen of stubborn burning up the hills.
Rough weather pricked the wind to lash the edges,
Sudden-shift the flames' direction, trap the men
Inside a ring of two thousand degrees.

The veterans rushed to build fire shelters while
The greens pickled in panic, lifting prayers

For helicopter rescue and the fire
Breaks they'd madly hacked to hold.
Gazing up through the swirling soot he watched
The sky not for salvation only, but
For a vision of his airborne years ahead.
When had he started to envision space,

Not just the blinking sky but heaven itself?
Hearing the word "Commander" by his name?
Emblazoning the echoless beyond?
Wragg, he remembered. Wragg had shot him there.

Clean water, filthy water, brackish, fresh,
Salt water, water the bestower of life,
Bringer of death, essence of bodily being,
Mother of the immaculate, father
Of poisonous mold, summoner of cockroaches,
Electronics destroyer, archive ruiner,

Reviver of the dying, element
Most princely of them all, most precious too,
Quiet culturer of cities, seed of thunder.
Mary had left behind her wish to fly.

The rocking of the waves would warm her blood.
Her scope had narrowed as her circle tightened,
Fading out most anyone but herself.
Craig called her not so often now. Friends like
Denise were cartoon faces on the phone—
Which she consulted less and less as hours

And days and weeks and months upon the water
Silted up inside her chest and skull.

Worked herself raw, nursed patience as the rising
Waters normalized the tunnel floods
That after a while crawled off the headline crawls.
And where the waters penetrated, soon
The ferries followed. Subway operators
Gushed onto the new lines as deckhands, bumped

The most experienced deckhands and ambitious
Engineers to captain all the bright new
Freshly christened boats veining the Apple
Festooned with rowdy crowds of workers deemed

Essential by the powers slicing in
And lording it from their icy porcelain skin.
No longer did ascending to the bridge
Demand so-many-hundred days aboard.
You knew the routes, could dock without mishap
Most of the time—yours was a Captain's chair.

From Myrtle Beach to Sheepshead Bay they sailed,
The Privateers of Waccamaw, hot for

A job and a cool breeze, the sweet relief
Of merely semi-tropical New York.
Ancestral, too, was old Brooklyn to some,
Though had they sought their Great-Greats they'd have found
Abandoned muddy fields that drained anew
With every plain-as-pound-cake summer storm.

They'd formed new families, though, like colonies
Of algae; sloshed their furry arms across
The wet, clawed at the main, swiping supplies,
Bemoaning the extinction of the squid.

New York infused this band of buccaneers
With hope for finer things. The sparkling town
Beamed them a private welcome, so it seemed—
The torch atop the Lady of the Harbor,
The lowing of the mighty Disney liners,
The crackling of the fires at Lemon Creek.

*I never thought I'd be an islander.*
*Inland childhood, mountain school.* She'd always

Craned upward for her future. Hard now though
To picture ever leaving these high harbors,
These spiky islands puffing up between,
These startling efflorescences of green,
The engine's roar under the Brooklyn Bridge,
The delicate steer to manage tricky docks.

After a few months filling in all around—
This boat and that boat, one line then the next—

She'd earned—or got by luck, was hard to tell—
A steady shift: daytimes, the Gateway Route.

And usually, a tub called *Happy Day.*
A grande dame of the fleet, one of the first,
She perked up under Mary's military-
Style command. *Leadership lessons not*
*Forgotten, no. Bailed out of school with something*
*Usable at least.* One long, three short,

And one more run now underway—Sunday,
So tourists mostly—down Jamaica Bay.

A golden sheen rose blinking off the water.
Black cormorants cruised low for silvery fish.
A party boat cut dangerously close,
Forced her to swerve nearly out of the channel.
But skill and instinct coalesced. She almost
Smiled, almost cracked her thickening shell.

After just two or three long days she felt
They'd bonded in a meeting of the minds.
Wragg, *Happy Day*, united under one
Flag: *1625*, orange and blue.

Demand high, talent scarce, the powers that be
Soon jettisoned the duty limits. Mary
Volunteered apace for extra shifts,
Then scored the pills that kept her catalyzed
('Twas righteous easy round these watery ways),
Disdained ship's coffee, ate them with a Coke.

One Monday in December, dawn snapped with
A sprinkle of snow and a MARSEC Level 2.

The online scuttlebutt spoke of attacks
On private craft by—wait for it—by pirates.
Rumors flew every day every which way,
Misinformation grew like mold on cheese—
But DHS set MARSEC levels, and
A 2 meant something more than phantom fears.

Snow cloaked the way ahead, the side-to-side,
The barges and the bridges and the birds.
Old-timers' memories of iced-up rivers
Hung in, unmelted by ten ice-free years,

But to the mostly youngster ferry crews
Snow on the water was a minor wonder.
One captain told of spotting seals up by
North Brother Island. Staring off the piers
At Wall Street by *Happy Day's* berth, our Wragg
Imagined open ocean lay before her.

The sun, invisible, slouched low over
Where Brooklyn Heights would be.

Cold flakes frosted her hair (shorn closer since
She'd mounted to a seat of authority,
Though still untameably spice-yellow
Like an almost setting sun, a bobbing buoy

Of hope on leaden waters) but archaic
Thoughts fizzed in her lizard brain, tiny
And faintly rank, fermenting unacknowledged.
Commuters lined up grimly for the run,

Fresh cloudy daylight trickling through grey pores,
Some clutching thermos coffee, others keen

To snag a cup of nasty ferry joe
And a muffin wrapped in planet-decimating

Clear crinkly plastic that echoed the hiss
Of jagged cranial sparks behind blue eyes
Pinkened with syrup of the highest fructose
And knocked askew by caffeinated brooding,
Dug extra deep by interrupted sleep,
Burn-blackened by snow's blank sublimity.

Slick Luz headed her gentle crew today.
"He popped the question! Look!" Luz flashed the ring.
"Now you can marry us right here on the boat,
Right, Captain?" "Sorry, wish it worked that way."

Of course Mary had looked this up. "You need
A real officiant. Maritime license
Is just for maritime." "Right—marry-time!
No?" Horned a laugh, elbowed Mary's ribs,
Peeled off to onboard passengers. Mary
Again scanned side-to-side and straight ahead.

*A normal run. A normal day. It's just*
*A little snow. No different from Upstate,*

*Or Colorado Springs. Happy Day* seemed
Ungainly-large this morning though,
Her dockage marrow-thin. From up the bridge
The view felt safer. This was no great storm,

Only a mild pre-Christmas snowfall called

Upon to pretty up the docks, hide the
Decay simpering up the towers' foundations.
Slowly those closest to the shore
Crept through their final days before old Chaos
Returned to jumble down their glass and steel.

Those monuments of capitalist greed
Lay off to port as Mary blew the horn,
Snuggling their witchy warrens like shorebirds
Husbanding precious eggs, blurring together,
Mythical still to a transplanted Upstater.
*Happy Day,* oblivious, motored soft under Wragg's wings

Into the white and grey, her sure bulk sliding
Slippery-armed at Brooklyn, and the fog

Began to lift, the dancing snow to lighten.
The weather meant no pleasure craft today,
A boon with visibility lopped short,
So, blinking blood-throbs back into her temples,
Wragg pushed the prow with sharklike confidence
Ahead toward the pink towers of DumboTech.

A little snow was nothing to a girl
Of three semesters at the Academy.
*Governors Island*, where had risen onetime
Coney Island rides. In winter School

Of Climate Studies kids rode in.
A girl had power to overcome. A girl
Had ribs as sturdy as any crewcut man's.
*Sharps Landing*, where a huge Ikea once
Had sucked in by the thousands local kids,
Artists, and families burgeoning with babes.

Through the rear bridge windows: a few stalwart
Souls braved the slippery snowy upper deck—

A father and two little girls, pink puffs
With Yankees hats, leaping and marveling
At what, she guessed, was their first-ever snow.
Girls who could grow to claim a Captain's chair.

*Industry City*, now a trivial walk
For disembarkers. Mostly just a Sam's Club—
The second-busiest in America.
A woman on a mission can't be stopped;
She finds her channel, code, or trail,
Her seasons and ambitions live, rotate,

Pile on, yes, die—and still Persephone
Ever re-mushrooms under still-blue sky.

*Bay Ridge's* Arab Spring bloomed all the year,
Her minarets already grey with age,
Her merchants of *halal* streaked with gold sweat.
Today a ferry, humble, pure of heart.
Next day a huge pan-Arctic cargo ship,
Even an ocean liner, town afloat.

*Fort Hamilton*, the infrastructure hub
Of Brooklyn, staffed with army engineers,
Housing the unhoused overflow still scurrying
Three confounding centuries on.

The world's a girl, a seed, potent; a vine,
Milky, full-flexed; an elm, transpendant.
A girl's the world, spinning, spitting sparks.
Overalls, ballet shoes, and in winter puffs

Of pink or purple. Parting the misty sea.
Fortress of knee and elbow, throne of thorns.

To *Coney Island*, thin spit, ghost of sweet-
Glorious, giddy, grimy carnival

Of old, patrolled by dolphins, nibbled at
By plovers, pipers, purple-turtle pods,
Coasted summer and fall with primates perched
On boards of foam and fiberglass—
Hushed fragile spectacles minute as men
Amid the stars. A solitary girl

Can sing a shark to sleep, then serve it up
For shipboard Christmas dinner or a feast
To celebrate Evacuation Day.
Whatever you hit her with, she can ferment

And fling back at you and at all the world.
*Marine Park*, route's end. Mary'd nearly missed
The angle in a couple times, so feeding
Extra attention in the air so thick.
Speed very low, toward the dock, awaiting
The land that should emerge amid the grey.

A deeper grey materialized to port,
A shrouded shape she chalked up to the kinks

Of vision she'd hid craftily before
The grouchy and distracted licensing
Examiners, her shipmates, and her crew.
Seven, ten seconds passed before it dawned
On Mary that this was no optic knot,
No mythic whale of creaky legend either.

A vessel, smaller, quicker than the ferry,
Topped with a late-built wooden tower to
Afford a height advantage, sheared in close,
Then very, then too close, and before she

Could even feel confused, much less react,
A *boom* and a horrible squeal bulleted up
From the below, *Happy Day* threw a shake,
*Well, holy fucking shit, they bumped us, do*
*They want to damage their own vessel too?*
No god of the deep offered a word of guidance.

Her temples froze about her spackled brain.
Four, no, five hooded primates, no, 'twas six
Leapt to the upper deck, grim tools in hand.
A thaw set in, her lizard brain whipped 'round

Only to face the black eye of a gun
Aimed through the frosty glass into the bridge.
"Kill the engine!" scratched a harsh bruised voice
"And no distress call!" Quivering like a fern,
Mary complied. The engine rumble died
And with it the embedded construct of

Free will that for the first time in her life
She felt was absolutely fundamental.

The tiny universe looked jittery,
Enstewed in crimson aspic. Mary's blood
Turned to dry ice, her innards to pink quartz.
The other pirates prodded the snowbirds

Off the upper deck, down to the main cabin
Like drops of bile swished down a bathroom drain;

Collected watches, wallets, purses, phones,
Sacked them up and re-emerged. Six minutes
Only, but to Captain Wragg a tortured
Century. Only a viscous minute more

And over the side they'd gone, and just like that
Begun to suavely motor off as if
After a friendly visitation. Wragg
Remained rapt, blocked, stone-solid-struck—

Until Luz poked her head up from below—
And spidering over and past her ran the man
Who'd had the two snow-loving little girls.
Stung to action Mary radioed in
A breathless phrase or two and then "Stand by."
Gusting into the bridge came Luz. "Nobody's hurt.

But this man's older daughter's missing."
"Get the police! The Coast Guard" shrieked the dad.

The pirate ship still moved off nonchalant;
Through the soft snowfall they watched her retreat.
The crew's rushed search had turned up not a sign.
The man. Stabbed with his finger. As if he.
Could. Strike up lightning. Like a god of storms.
"They took her." One by one and two by two,

Traumatized riders ventured up. Untrusting
Of her still-stunned visual memory
Mary demanded much too harshly if
He knew for sure. "Fuck! Where else could she be?"

"Help is on the way," she croaked. Faced forward,
Leaving the man, the crew, the passengers
To their own sores and panics. Ten seconds passed.
Then of their own free will her fingers stirred
The engine to its fine familiar growl.
Help could be half an hour away for all

They knew. She nosed her tiny shiny ship
Toward the attackers' craft, still just in sight

Heading towards the Breezy Point wetlands—
Where just a few stilt-housers stuck it out—
Beyond which lay the Bight, where Flight 800
Lay in its murky grave, and open sea.

At last Keith's tour wrapped up, at last, at last,
Anina's favorite, Craig's beloved son,

Cristina's all-adored. Yolanda's hands,
Raw-reddened from rebuilding, yanked him in.
Smell of fresh paint, a cheap new easy chair
(Half-price at Sam's Club), drywall hastily

Replaced along the half-sunk back rooms where
The water'd smashed its worst. And in the yard
The strawberry plants, devoutly tended by
Young Nathan once, now re-dispersed across
The vaporous Universe. Winter had come
But it yet felt like autumns Keith remembered.

Settling in, he found it hard to sleep,
Mired in milk-quiet claustrophobia.

That Saturday, Yolanda free, kids home
From school, he swept them into the white Ford
Explorer, spit them out into bright blue
Scuffed plastic kayaks on the blustery lake.

He and the girl in one, his wife and son
Taking another, out they arced into
The sloppy-wet, almost-warm country air.
Keith rowed. Cristina gazed into the sky
Criss-crossed by contrails. *Orange seaplane!*
"Coming down, look, Dad! I want to ride

In one of those! Can we? Can I ride
In one of those?" "Darn right, darn right you can.

Next spring, promise. The sky's the limit
For you, kid. You're my sweet girl in the sky."
"What are you telling her?" Yolanda called.
Keith and Cristina smiled, pretended not
To hear. No, Mama's boat was just too far.
The seaplane down, a holy quiet reigned

Once more over the magic lake whose ripply
Surface stretched to kiss the hills and sky.

No child would be kidnapped on Mary's watch.
Passengers boiled up and down till Luz
Swept them all squawking to the lower deck.
The two male crewmen searched lifejacket bins
Again, the bathrooms, any hiding place,
Panicking quietly, fearing for their jobs

And for the little missing girl, of course—
Whose sister cried and father paced and spun
His shorn head nearly off his shoulders, spearing
His eyes and, as he felt, his soul itself

Into every last crevasse, shadow, murk,
Refusing to imagine—Mary, though,
Scalded with rage, bathed in regret, impelled
By what? She could not name it—
Was driven by a vision of a girl
Stolen by evil men, images rattling

Loose her own livid red memory chips.
One dark-eyed crewman crept inside the bridge.

"Where are we heading!?" Mary couldn't look
Into him. *If they took that girl then we*
*Are gonna get her back.* "Just get below,
And keep the passengers below." The boy

Retreated to the deck, slipped, caught himself
On a cold metal chair—the snow now just
A glinting trickle, goddess of the morning
Showing her gauzy face, enemy now
A straight clear shot ahead. She spurred the boat
To knife the water faster than it should.

Too late she saw the buoy that marked the spot
Where just three years before an ancient barge
Had burst aflame and sunk into the muck
Tail up. A moment later, gashed, roughly

A-spin and a-wobble, *Happy Day* gasped,
Destined to join her. Sprawled across her chair,

Our Mary heard her heart pounding like thunder,
But couldn't move another muscle as
The panic-blooming passengers stumbled
Around the deck. A Coast Guard boat swung into
View, an NYPD craft beside.
The scrambling shouting rescue game began.

*I am the Captain. Yes, I wrecked the boat.*
*Still I'm the Captain.* Mary shuddered up
To help, to guide the passengers over
The side into the bobbing rescue craft.

The cops and Coast Guard crew labored like ants
And sooner than she had imagined all
Were safe, two dozen passengers decamped.
Her two crewmen went last, Luz must have gone
As well, Luz would be married soon, *That's nice,*
*So nice for her, oh, wouldn't it be fun*

*If I really could marry them on board.*
A smile tried to slip-crack across her face.

Little girl lost loomed large and Wragg
Refracted back into the bridge cabin,
Lost balance, hit the floor beside her chair,
Felt seasick, her eyes spinning counterwise

To *Happy Day's* death spiral. From down here
Shadows sheared her from the outside world
Of water, light, and love. The ferry had
But moments left afloat. And Wragg was Captain.
And Captain she would stay, the kidnapped girl
Fired far away, a missile in the sky.

Wragg had to be reborn to e'er begin
To face the father and the discipline.

Dragging a chilled pink puff, Luz struggled toward
The rescue craft that lingered as close by
As safety would allow. Tumbling rocklike
Into the bay, she waved and called and found
A lifebuoy to grasp. The girl had seen
The guns, shuffled deep as she could into

A corner cabinet, passed out from panic,
Clenched there until Luz took one last late look.
Now hands reached to pull both out of the waves
And a crushed father melted with relief.

And what a tale he'd always have to tell—
But not yet, and not to his mates at school,
Who might squint at him sideways at the image
Of Ladykiller Dover begging rescue
From hellfire in the woods of Oregon.
Instead he bore down on his PDFs

On astroengineering, and on clear
Nights in his boots he'd stare up at the stars

And wonder if the space program would take him
And wonder at how many stars there were
And wonder why the girls meant so damn little
And wonder at the space-age architecture

And wonder—whatever became of Wragg
Who burned in him sometimes like a sore muscle?

One whom he'd truly liked had liquified.
"Oh, well. Love ain't for keeping," Dover sighed.

THE
End